Weekly Reader Children's Book Club presents

MONSTERS
AND OIL WELLS
DON'T MIX

Illustrated by Gilbert Riswold

MONSTERS AND OIL WELLS DON'T MIX

by Wilma Pitchford Hays

Xerox Education Publications

XEROX

To David, Stephen and Susanna

Publishing, Executive, and Editorial Offices:
Xerox Education Publications
Middletown, Connecticut 06457

ISBN   0-88375-213-1

Library of Congress Catalog Card Number: 76-13783

Weekly Reader Children's Book Club Edition
XEROX® is a trademark of Xerox Corporation.

Contents

1

A Mysterious Footprint

Lon Adams ran along the path that bordered the cypress swamp. Near a black pool of water where he often fished for bream, a squirrel dropped from a tree, sat up and begged.

"I remembered," Lon said and tossed a peanut to it.

The squirrel snatched it, ran up a tree and began to eat. Lon laughed happily, for Grandpa Regan had said that an animal only took food from someone it trusted.

Lon and his twin sister, Laurie, had made friends of many animals since Grandpa had brought them to live in his motor home near this isolated Florida swamp. Only yesterday they had found a large footprint of some strange creature on the beach. He wished he knew what had made it.

He reached the beach and saw Laurie, as suntanned as he in her bathing suit. She was kneeling on the wet sand.

"Did you find another strange footprint?" he called.

"No," Laurie answered, "but I caught a monster horseshoe crab."

Lon knelt beside the light-brown crab which Laurie held on the sand by its dagger-shaped tail. "It's a big one, a foot across," Lon said. "Turn it over so we can see its eyes better."

Gently Laurie turned the crab onto its humped back and watched six pairs of claw-tipped legs wave back and forth.

"I read that horseshoe crabs have such extraordinary eyes," Lon said, "that scientists are studying them to learn how to make electronic computers 'see' better."

"Their eyes look like beads to me," Laurie said.

"Let it go now," Lon said. "We don't want to hurt it."

She flipped the crab over and it scuttled into the Gulf water.

"It's suppertime," Lon said and they left the beach, walking single file along the path where he had fed the squirrel. He tried to see deeper into the trees. Anything could live in such an ancient wilderness. He wished he could explore it, but Grandpa had warned them not to go far into the swamp.

"You could get lost in there," he had said.

Grandpa Regan was like a father to them, for

8

Lon and Laurie saw their own father only when he came home on vacations. He worked on the Alaska pipeline in territory too icy and rugged to take his family.

Grandpa, too, had been a wildcat oil driller for thirty years, finding oil for a big petroleum company. Now he was exploring for oil for himself with several partners. One of them was his daughter, Alice Adams, Laurie and Lon's mother.

As they reached the motor home, they heard Grandpa under the outside shower he had rigged with a barrel on a pole. The sun heated the barrel so that water felt warm to them when they showered, but Grandpa sputtered as if icewater trickled down on him.

Laurie grinned. "You can always *hear* when Grandpa's home," she said.

"Lon," he shouted from inside the circle of shower curtain, "I left my towel hanging on the fence around your duck pen."

Lon got the towel and took it to him. Grandpa stuck his head out between the curtains and dried his graying black hair.

"Your ducks were making an awful fuss when I came home," he said. "I thought they were thirsty and took water to them, but their pan wasn't empty."

Lon frowned. Before he got out of bed this morning he had heard his six pet ducks quacking in fear. He thought a stray dog or fox might be bothering them, but when he went to their pen, nothing was there. He had to talk to them several minutes before they settled down.

"Something scares them" he said. "Do you think there could be bears living in the swamp?"

"Never heard of any," Grandpa said, "but I did find the remains of a raccoon near my drilling rig. Takes a good sized animal to kill and eat a full-grown raccoon."

Lon was still wondering what had frightened his ducks as he climbed the kitchen steps of the large motor home. His mother was writing at the small dining table.

"What's for supper?" he asked.

His mother smiled. "Always starving!" she said. "Why don't you make hamburgs while Laurie fixes a salad? I have to record today's core samples."

He looked over her shoulder at several damp piles of sand spread on brown paper. They didn't look oily to him. "Any luck?" he asked.

She shook her head. Lon knew she was worried, for the holder on the wall still held unpaid bills. This was the second dry well Grandpa had drilled on the land he had leased. Drilling wells cost a lot of money, even though the men who worked with Grandpa were partners and worked on shares.

"What makes Grandpa so sure he will strike oil," Lon asked, "when the big oil companies gave up here ten years ago?"

Grandpa overheard and shouted from his bed-
room, "Nothing the matter with my wells, Boy,
that a little oil couldn't cure."

He came into the kitchen buttoning his clean
plaid shirt. "Ned and I drilled here for the company ten years ago," he said.

Lon nodded. Ned Lonley was Grandpa's geologist
partner. Lon had been named for him.

"Well, Ned believed there was oil here ten years
ago," Grandpa said, "and I believe it. After nine
dry wells, the company ordered us to abandon drilling. I think we just didn't drill deep enough. We've
better equipment today."

Grandpa always talked to him and Laurie as if
he expected them to go into business with him
someday, as their mother had, and he wanted
them to know something about it.

"Are you going to drill a third well?" Lon asked.

"We will if we can lease the land next to mine
before one of the big companies gets it ahead of
us. Ned is trying to raise more money now. Several
men who worked with us years ago, retired now,
have agreed to put their savings into the deal."

Lon hoped that Grandpa's friends wouldn't lose
their money along with his. Exploring for oil was
risky, even though Grandpa Regan was one of the
best wildcat drillers in the country.

"Aren't we going to get any supper around

here?" Grandpa asked.

"As soon as you get the newspaper," Lon said, for Grandpa had to drive three miles for it to the rural mailbox on the nearest highway.

He left, and Lon took hamburg from the refrigerator. Laurie came in from the garden with green onions in her hand.

"I saw a large footprint in the earth between the rows of onions," she said. "It was big—really big! Do you think it might be the creature that scared your ducks?"

Lon looked carefully at her to see if she was teasing. She was the practical, down-to-earth twin, while he couldn't help letting his imagination run away with him at times. She seemed honestly puzzled.

"Was it the pawprint of an animal?" he asked finally.

"Not any animal I ever saw," Laurie said.

"I've got to see it," Lon said. "Come on."

Together they ran down the kitchen steps into the garden and leaned over the giant print.

"It's a big foot or paw," Lon agreed. "It seems to have four toes going out from a large round center. See?"

"Maybe wind blew sand from the pawprint of a large stray dog," Laurie suggested. "I've heard that wind can make prints grow wider and bigger."

"Maybe," Lon said, but he didn't believe it.

12

The wind had not frightened his ducks. Something real had made them quack in fear. The wind had not killed and eaten the grown raccoon that Grandpa had seen. What strange creature lived in the tangle of trees and vines and swamp beside their motor home?

2

Something Was Here

Lon and Grandpa went to their twin bunks across the aisle from the room where Mother and Laurie slept. Laurie turned off the lights but left the door open so they could continue talking about the footprint in the garden.

"I know the print of a bear's paw," Grandpa said. "That wasn't a bear."

"I think Laurie is right," Mother said. "The wind enlarged the pawprint of a big stray dog."

"I've been reading about strange creatures that lived long ago," Lon said. "Horseshoe crabs haven't changed in millions of years. Armadillos, who dig up our yard at night for grubs, are as old. So are the alligators we see in the swamp. Maybe there are monsters surviving in the woods, deep, where no one ever sees them."

"Oh, Lon," Laurie said. "Someone would have seen a monster if it lived here. We're only ten miles from a town with lots of people."

Lon ignored her. "Remember that Abominable Chicken Man you told us about, Grandpa?" he asked. "You said it walked like a gorilla and tore hinges off chicken houses and stole a rancher's chickens—when you worked in Oklahoma."

"Ned was the one who saw the footprints," Grandpa said. "Ned said he quit laughing at that rancher's story real quick. Said he wouldn't want to meet anything that size in the woods!"

Lon lay wide awake thinking that he wouldn't want to meet it either. In the dark it was easy to believe that some creature from long ago might still live in the deep swamp beside their motor home. If there was something, he wished he could see it—if it didn't see him.

He must have slept. He didn't know how long. The quacking of the ducks waked him. His heart beat hard as he listened for the sound of something that might have frightened them, maybe the barking of a dog or grunt of a wild boar.

The ducks quacked louder. He had to help them. Barefoot, he ran to the high fence that he and Grandpa had built to protect his pets. In the dim light from a quarter-moon, he saw the white ducks running back and forth, flapping their wings in terror. Nothing was chasing them.

He hooked his fingers through the strong steel links of the fence and called, "Quiet. You'll wake everybody."

16

They were too frightened to come as they usually did when he talked to them. He started for the gate.

Then he saw something move at the edge of the swamp, not ten feet from him. A big hairy shape.

Lon couldn't yell. He couldn't move. He looked up into the dark, almost human face of something bigger than Grandpa. It stood on two legs like a man and stared at him as if it wondered what *he* was. Then it turned and moved off, in no hurry, into the swamp trees.

Something that big doesn't need to hurry, Lon thought. Who would chase it?

Grandpa called from the kitchen door, "Lon, where are you? What's the matter with those ducks?"

Lon ran to the house. "A monster," he gasped. "A live monster with a dark, man-like face. It didn't try to hurt me."

His mother and Laurie came and turned on the outdoor spotlight.

"Lon," Mother said, "I knew all that talk about footprints and the Abominable Chicken Man would give you nightmares."

"It wasn't a nightmare," Lon said. "Ducks don't have nightmares. They knew. And I saw it."

"Oh, Lon!" Laurie said. "Next you'll say it had green hair and red eyes."

"Come," Lon said, "maybe there are footprints."

17

They followed Grandpa, who carried a flashlight and swung its beam from side to side over the ground. There were no prints on the brown pine needles that carpeted the edge of the swamp. No prints beside the duck pen where the earth was hard and dry. The ducks were huddled now in one corner against the wire.

"Lon," his mother said, "you've always had a vivid imagination. Maybe you saw a shadow as a cloud passed over the moon."

He didn't know how he was going to convince her that this time it had not been a creature of his imagination. Then Grandpa Regan gave a surprised whistle.

Everyone turned and saw the beam from his flashlight playing along the fence. The top wire was crumpled as if something had leaned on it. They ran to inspect it closely.

18

"Something was here," Grandpa said. "Something powerful, to bend a fence like that."

For a long moment no one spoke. Then Laurie said, "Lon, you weren't exaggerating. What can it be?"

"Didn't we read in the newspaper," his mother asked, "that a gorilla had escaped from a circus near here this summer?"

"This wasn't a gorilla," Lon said. "It walked like a man."

"There are times," Mother said, "when I wish we lived near a telephone line."

"Tomorrow when the men come from town to work," Grandpa said, "I'll send word to the County Animal Control officers. This is something they'll want to investigate."

3
Exploring
for
Oil

Lon was wakened the next morning by Grandpa talking to the two men who worked with him. Pete and Bill Martin stopped every morning to take Grandpa to the oil rig.

"Print isn't too clear," Grandpa was saying from the garden. "It faded during that heavy dew last night. What do you make of it?"

Pete said, "A horse without a shoe could have stepped here. Heard of a stray horse about?"

Lon got out of bed and dressed quickly. He knew it wasn't a horse. He hadn't thought of wind and dew wiping out the only evidence he had to show the officers from Animal Control.

When he came to the kitchen, Laurie was eating breakfast. His mother, in jeans and shirt, stood at the counter sipping a cup of coffee before going to the rig.

"Grandpa says the print is fading," Lon said. "We've got to do something. It's our only proof."

"In that book we're reading about fossils," Laurie said, "the scientists soaked burlap bags in flour paste and let them dry hard to hold the shape of skulls and bones they moved."

"That won't work for us," Lon said, "if we push a bag into the print, we'll really mess it up."

"I know," Laurie said. "Remember our school beach picnic? We dug the shape of flowers in the wet sand, then filled them with liquid plaster. When they dried, they came out perfect."

"That's not a bad idea," Lon said. "Trouble is— that was special plaster the teacher brought. We don't have anything to fill the prints with."

Their mother put down her coffee cup. "When I was a kid," she said, "we used to make our own plaster stuff to fill molds. We shredded newspapers and mixed them with a little flour and water to make a paste."

"We could make that," Laurie said.

"It's worth trying," Lon agreed. "We have to have something to show the officers. If they're busy, they may not come for several days. The print could be gone by then."

All morning they experimented to get the right mixture of bits of newspaper and paste in a big kettle. At last they pressed the gray paste carefully into the blurred print in the garden, then stood back to look at it.

"It's like a blob of cement somebody dropped,"

Laurie said in dismay.

"Wait until the sun bakes it," Lon urged. "When we lift it, it will show the print."

Late in the afternoon the plaster cast had dried and Laurie lifted it carefully. She turned it over, brushed off the dirt and frowned.

"It's still only a blob," she said.

Lon had to agree, "At least the men can see the size of it," he said.

When Pete and Bill Martin brought Grandpa home, Lon took the cast to their pickup truck. "Will you take this to town to show the Animal Control officers?" he asked.

"What is it?" Pete asked.

"A cast of the creature's footprint," Lon said.

"That's going to impress them!" Bill said.

Both men were grinning as if the print was a big joke. Lon wished they had seen what he had seen at the duck pen last night.

Grandpa got out of the truck and slammed its door. "You keep an eye on that Tate fellow," he cautioned the men. "Tate's no reason to be in this area unless he's up to something."

Lon wondered who Tate was and what he had done to upset Grandpa.

"Tate and I were roustabouts together in the Texas oilfields," Pete said. "He's a tough egg!"

"Then we'll scramble him," Grandpa shouted as they drove away. He grinned, enjoying his joke.

Lon laughed, too, walking toward the house with Grandpa. "What tough egg are you going to scramble? And why?" he asked.

"Trevor Tate," Grandpa answered. "Tate showed up in town a few days ago and asked Pete how we were doing out here. Exploring for oil is like prospecting for gold. Every oil scout hopes to beat the other man to leases in good oil territory. We don't have the money to lease all the land around here. We have to wait until we're pretty sure of oil before we pay the owners for rights to take oil from under their lands."

"You mean," Lon said, "Mr. Tate is watching you to see if you strike oil, so he can hurry to sign leases on the land before you can?"

"That's about it," Grandpa said. "Pete saw Tate snooping near our rig after dark when he thought he couldn't be seen."

"He didn't learn much," Lon said. "Your well turned out to be dry."

"Maybe the next one won't," Grandpa said. "Just one strike is all we need, Lon."

Grandpa Regan's eyes were shining. When he talks about oil, Lon thought, he's like a man finding gold or diamonds. Of course oil was scarce and he wanted to help overcome the energy crisis, but there was more than that.

Grandpa loved the excitement of sniffing out the right places to drill, never knowing when a great black gusher of crude would spout from the earth where his drill bit had gone through thousands of feet of layered sand and shale. He was always looking forward to that moment when the drill bit would crumble the crust over an oil trap that had formed millions of years ago. He had told Lon and Laurie that oil was made when marine plants and animals had died and changed slowly into drops of oil to be soaked up by porous rock as a sponge soaks up water.

Lon was feeling some of Grandpa's excitement. "If we make a strike," he asked, "will we form our own oil company?"

"No, processing crude oil takes millions of dollars," Grandpa Regan said. "Only a big company can afford to handle the transporting by pipeline, or truck or rail or ocean tankers. Then crude has to be refined and manufactured into all kinds of fuel for different purposes."

"I know," Lon said. "Jet fuel, regular gasoline, unleaded gas, diesel fuel. Kerosene. Oil for furnaces. Greases and lubricating oil. Bottled gas like we use in the motor home."

"That's only a beginning," Grandpa said. "All kinds of things are made from oil—tires and clothing and footballs."

"Oil runs power plants for lights and air-conditioning and manufacturing," Lon added. "No wonder we could run out of oil."

"I only want to *find* oil," Grandpa said, " and I'm pretty good at that. Any big company will rush to buy our leases if we get a whiff of crude. We make our living re-selling leases for more than we paid for them."

They stopped at the outdoor shower and Grandpa went in, talking through the curtain. "We have to make our strike first. I hope it's soon."

Lon knew by the tone of his voice that Grandpa was in trouble if he didn't find oil this time.

4

Pranksters

Two nights later Lon lay in bed and listened to Grandpa and Mother talking with Ned Lonley, their geologist partner. They sat at the kitchen table and studied reports of core samples taken at different depths in the well Grandpa was drilling.

"I believe the oil is there," Ned said. "How great is the risk?"

Lon knew they were trying to decide whether to start a new well or dig deeper into the present one. The deeper they drilled, the greater the risk that their string of heavy drilling tools and pipe might drop to the bottom of a hole. If this happened they could lose the well and expensive tools.

"We've got to take the risk and drill deeper," Grandpa said finally. "I can smell oil, I tell you."

They were still talking when Lon fell asleep. When he waked, all three of them had gone to the rig.

As he and Laurie were washing their breakfast

dishes, they heard a truck pull into the yard beside the motor home. Lon went to the kitchen door. The truck was marked ANIMAL CONTROL. Its entire back end was a strong wire mesh cage.

One of the two officers left the truck and came to Lon. "We're looking for Chuck Regan. Is he home?" he asked.

"No. Grandpa's working," Lon said.

"We have a report of a strange creature in the swamp bush here," he said. "Are you the boy who claimed to see it?"

"Yes," Lon said.

He was glad the officer did not ask to go see Grandpa, who didn't want visitors near his drilling rig. Today he'd be particularly irritable with the risks he was taking.

"I'll show you where I saw something," Lon said. "Right out by the duck pen."

Laurie came with them. "I found the monster print in the garden," she said. "Did you get the cast we made?"

"We got a gob made of newspaper and paste," the officer said drily.

"There's hardly a trace of that print now," Lon said.

He and Laurie led the two officers to the duck pen. Lon told them about seeing the monster face to face. "Grandpa took a crowbar and straightened the fence," he said, "but you can see where it was bent."

The men looked closely but said nothing. One of them stepped into the trees at the edge of the swamp, head bent, searching for a sign that a large animal had been there.

The other walked the opposite way to a small spring which trickled into the woods and finally disappeared into the cypress swamp. The spongy earth gave way under his feet and he leaped back onto dry land. Then he stopped and called to the other officer.

"Something big crushed these ferns. Not many hours ago, either. They haven't wilted."

Laurie and Lon ran ahead of the second officer, who knelt and examined the broken ferns.

"Could have been that a deer hid her fawn," he said. "Maybe a black bear or a bobcat. This swamp is wild enough to harbor any of them."

"We've seen wildcat, deer and raccoons," Lon said, "but never a black bear."

"How big are black bears?" Laurie asked.

The first officer had moved down the stream into the trees. He called again. "None of those animals made *this* track."

Lon and Laurie stared in disbelief at the huge print of a foot in the muddy bank of the stream.

"It's a single track," the officer said, "clear and deep. Must be fourteen inches long and six across."

"That's bigger than the one in the garden," Lon almost whispered as if the "thing" could hear him. "Could there be two creatures?"

"Could be," the officer said, "but the print smells like a rat to me. There's been a lot of talk in town since you sent in that cast. Some prankster might have planted this print here."

"You mean someone would make that print — just to get people excited?" Lon asked.

"Sure," the officer said. "Some folks get their kicks out of playing practical jokes on others. Must have been a dozen cars followed us out this way to see exactly where we were going. Curious people hunting excitement. But we put up a roadblock where your Grandpa's private trail leaves the high-way."

"A roadblock will only stop their cars," the second officer said. "It will take them awhile to walk in here."

"Or remove the block!" the other said.

"I hope we're not going to have a lot of visitors," Lon said. "Grandpa won't like that. A careless person can easily set fire to an oil well."

"How could someone make a print like that?" Laurie asked. "How do you know it isn't real?"

"I don't," the officer said, "but it's just a little too deep and clear, as if someone pressed a big fishing boot into the mud, a boot with something wrapped around it to make it look bigger and more

31

like a paw."

Laurie nodded. "If it had been a monster," she said, "where could it go from here? Only one print. Nothing else disturbed."

Lon knew that his sister was probably right to accept the practical answer, but he *felt* something here. He stared into the thicket of cypress trees. Underneath these were high fern and deep bush. Vines crept up trunks and through branches. The creature could have swung into the trees on a strong vine.

"I'd like to know for sure what it was," he said.

"Tell you what," an officer said as they returned to the control truck. "If you see or hear anything again, send us word at once. "We'll drop whatever

we're doing and come right out here.

"Telephone lines don't come this far into the woods," Lon said, "but Grandpa could drive in and tell you."

"Fine," the officers said, and smiled at each other as they drove away.

Lon watched them go. He wasn't sure that they had believed anything he told them. Maybe they thought he was the prankster and it was all a hoax.

He walked with Laurie toward the motor home and saw a young woman sitting on the kitchen steps. A man was at the duck pen taking photographs. Laurie joined the visitor on the steps while Lon ran to the pen.

"You the kid that saw the swamp-ape?" the man asked.

"I saw *something*," Lon said.

"I'm a reporter," the man said. "Stand by the fence and point to the spot you saw it."

He was so forceful that Lon obeyed him without thinking. The man snapped a picture.

"Now what about the footprint?" he asked.

"The first one faded," Lon answered. "We found another today, but the officers say it was probably made by a prankster."

The reporter was immediately interested. "We'll judge that for ourselves," he said. "Where is it?"

Lon took him to the huge clear print in the mud.

"Only one," he said. "The officers say it is too perfect to be true."

The reporter didn't seem to think so. He took several close-up photographs and hurried away.

"Watch for your picture in the newspaper," he called back to Lon.

Lon went to the house and found Laurie making a cup of coffee for the young woman who now sat at the kitchen table. She smiled when Lon sat down across from her.

"I'm Jane Kimball," she said, "from the University of Tampa. I heard about the ape-man you saw and came to see it, too, if I can."

"I never said ape-man," Lon said, "or swamp-ape either The officers called it that. I did see something very large and hairy. It had a dark hairless face, more human than ape, I think. It stood and walked like a man."

Jane leaned forward, fascinated. "Your description agrees with the prospector, Ostman, who was kidnapped by such a monster in 1924. Did you ever read Ostman's story?"

"No," Lon said. Did she think he was making up a tale like something he had read?

"I'm writing a Master's thesis on strange creatures or monsters seen over the years in America," Jane said. "This is the closest I've ever come to a real sight of one. I hope I see him."

Lon looked at her. Jane Kimball wore jeans and

a blue t-shirt. She seemed young to be through college and working on her Master's degree. Her black hair was parted in the middle and hung long and straight, held back by a beaded band as an Indian girl might wear it. Her gray eyes were as eager as Grandpa's when he talked about oil.

Laurie brought her coffee and a doughnut. "Do you really believe there are monsters?" Laurie asked. "That something could have lived over many years in deep woods and swamps where people didn't see them?"

"I don't know," Jane said. "There are lots of things in nature which we can't explain. Scientists have found several 'living fossils' in the last few years."

"How can a fossil be alive?" Lon asked.

"That's what they call creatures of long ago who were believed to have all died," Jane explained. "But a few have actually survived and been seen recently. They are important living links to the past."

"I read about a fish," Lon said, "and a jungle sloth, and that tribe of cavemen in the Philippines."

"At least," Jane said, "I know enough not to say that anything *can't* be true."

Lon nodded, but Laurie still looked doubtful.

"I'll have to go now," Jane said. "It's quite a walk back to the road where I left my jeep. Do you think your family would mind if I camped overnight deep in the swamp? That's the only way I can hope to see it."

Lon was uneasy. Grandpa definitely didn't want strangers near in case he struck oil before the leases were signed on surrounding land. He said, "The swamp isn't ours. It belongs to the state."

"No one ever goes there, not even in the day-time," Laurie added. "It's swarming with mos-quitoes and snakes and alligators.

"I have bug repellent," Jane said. "Friends of mine from the University live in town. They'd help me build a platform in the trees to put my pup-tent on. I'd be okay up there in a sleeping bag."

Lon looked at her with respect. She was brave and resourceful.

"A tree-tent," he said. "I wish I could stay there overnight."

"Why not," Jane said, "if your mother will let you? It won't be big enough to stand up in, but we can sit and lie down. Have you sleeping bags?"

"Sure," Laurie said. "We'll ask Mother."

"Will you stop here on your way into the swamp tomorrow?" Lon asked.

"Yes," she said as she stood up to leave. "I wouldn't mind having company. I know you'd be very quiet and not frighten any creature away."

"We would," they promised.

They could scarcely wait until Mother and Grandpa and Ned came home. They heard the car and ran to meet it. Mother handed Lon a large package.

"I had to go into town," she said, "and the shrimp boats were in. So we'll have jumbo pink shrimp for supper."

While Mother boiled the shrimp and Grandpa showered, Lon and Laurie set the picnic table beside the motor home. It was beautifully shady there with a sea breeze to discourage the bugs and gnats.

"I love shrimp," Lon said, "and we're having French bread with herb butter. And watermelon

cold from the refrigerator. My favorite supper."

He put on extra paper napkins, for everyone would peel his own boiled shrimp.

"Maybe we better wait to ask to stay overnight with Jane," Laurie said, "until we've had supper. Mother is more likely to say yes if she is not hungry and tired."

"Okay," Lon said. "I'd sure like to sleep in a tree-tent."

As soon as they all sat down to eat, Lon told about the Animal Control officers coming and finding the large, too-perfect footprint.

"The officers decided that some prankster made this last print," Laurie said.

"Whatever for?" Mother said. "Who would want to frighten us?"

Grandpa was so disturbed that he quit eating the shrimp piled high before him. "I think I know who it was, and why," he said.

"Trevor Tate's guessed how near we are to striking oil. He'd like to get around to the land owners and buy leases before we can—if we do strike—but not until he's sure. If he can get us excited about a swamp monster—take our minds off our business—he gains more time to snoop around the rig and learn what we've got there."

"But the first print was real," Laurie said.

"That first real print probably gave him the idea," Mother said. "He had to hear about it. Everyone in town asked me questions today. They wanted to know if we had heard any more strange sounds or had seen anything again."

"I hope you told them we hadn't," Grandpa said. "We can't have strangers out here, careless with cigarettes and matches. All we need is a fire to wipe us out."

"After what we learned today," Ned said, "we don't want anyone around here before the Town Clerk's office opens on Monday."

Lon looked at Laurie. She seemed as troubled as he was. This was only Friday night. What would they do about Jane, who would be back tomorrow with her friends to put up a tree-tent in the swamp?

"If it was someone careful," Lon began.

Grandpa interrupted. "Nobody!" he said. "We trust no stranger until the leases are signed." Then he leaned forward and spoke softly, for him. "There's oil this time, kids. We drilled deeper today. I saw traces of oil in the mud and water we pumped up. We smelled gas, all of us. We're going to test tomorrow. We've got the Christmas tree ready to bolt her down if she comes."

Lon felt Grandpa's excitement. The Christmas tree was made of steel valves and controls, with arms that looked something like a tree. It was locked and bolted over the pipeline when pressure began to rise from the well, when something deep rumbled in the ground, trying to come up.

"Are you sure?" Lon asked.

"Sure enough to buy leases now," Ned said, "and it would have to be Friday night. Trevor Tate has all weekend to learn what we found and beat us to the landowners on Monday."

"Why don't you go to the landowners right now, tonight?" Lon said, "Or don't you have the money?"

"Ned raised enough money," Grandpa said, "but we have to get the list of landowners from the Town Clerk's office. If we had asked earlier for the names, Tate would have known we sniffed oil."

"I almost made it this afternoon," Mother said. "I ran all the way to Jim Carter's office but it had closed for the weekend."

"Is Mr. Carter the Town Clerk?" Laurie asked. "I play with Angie. Why don't you go to his house and get him to open the office? I'll bet he would if he knew how important it was for you to get the list now."

Grandpa put both hands on the table. He looked surprised, then smiled. "He might, at that," he said.

"Out of the mouths of babes," Ned said.

Mother got up and gave Lon a hug, then Laurie. She turned to Grandpa. "Ned and I will go right now," she said. "We'll each take our own car, so if we get the list, we can call on different landowners. Faster that way."

Grandpa nodded. "Pete and Bill are on duty at the rig tonight. I'll stay here in case we have visitors."

Lon knew "visitors" meant Trevor Tate, who wanted to buy land leases for his company before Grandpa could.

Mother had gone before Lon and Laurie remembered that they had not asked if they could stay overnight with Jane in the swamp tomorrow.

"Maybe she'll come back before tomorrow night," Laurie said.

"I hope so," Lon said.

He didn't want to miss the chance to see the strange monster that lived in the swamp, if one really lived there.

5

The
Hunt

Laurie woke Lon the next morning. "Grandpa went out early," she said, "and Mother didn't come home last night."

Lon sat up and pulled on his jeans. "Then she must have the list from the Town Clerk's office," he said. "She won't come home until she has signed up every landowner she can find."

"If she doesn't get home today," Laurie said, "we'll have to ask Grandpa if we can stay overnight in Jane's tree-tent. What if he says no?"

Suddenly they heard Grandpa shouting at someone in the yard, "Put out that fire!"

There was the sound of running feet. Young people's voices called, "Here! Get this one."

Lon and Laurie ran out the kitchen door. Grandpa was beating at flames that raced along the dry grass into the deep woods beside the road.

A half dozen young men and women were chasing narrow snakes of fire. Barebacked men were

trying to smother flames with their shirts. Jane was striking at a blaze with a red and blue plaid blanket.

By the time Lon reached them, they had won against the flames. What was left of the bonfire looked like a giant octupus, a round black center with eight smoking tenacles reaching toward the woods and the motor home.

"What are you doing here?" Grandpa shouted to

the cinder-grimed young people. "You could have burned down the whole place."

"I'm sorry," Jane said. "We were cooking breakfast when a gust of wind blew sparks everywhere."

"Get off my place," Grandpa said. "You're trespassing."

The boys and girls looked at each other as if they thought he was an old crab, especially after they had worked hard to put out the fire. Lon knew

45

what they didn't know, that a forest fire could have blown up Grandpa's oil well and all his hopes of a big strike.

"Grandpa, you've burned your hand," Laurie cried.

He held out his hands as if surprised at the blisters forming on the thumb and lower palm. He was so angry, he must not have felt the pain until now.

Jane ran and brought a first-aid kit from her back pack. "When I camp out," she said, "I have medicine for an emergency."

He winced but said nothing while she cleaned away the cinders with a cotton swab soaked in lotion.

Laurie and Lon watched as Jane wrapped the blistered hand in a gauze bandage. "Loosely," she said, "just to keep the dirt from getting to it."

"You're a good nurse," Grandpa said. "Thank you."

From the woods a man called, "Someone's going to get shot, if you don't put that rifle away."

Another man answered, "I came here to shoot that ape. I've got a hunting license and the right to use my gun."

A uniformed officer wearing a badge came to Grandpa. "I'm Lieutenant Raff," he said. "The sheriff sent me out to control the curiosity seekers. After the newspaper came out, we knew you'd

46

have a mob here."

"We haven't seen the newspaper," Lon said.

The lieutenant reached into his back pocket and handed them the local four-page paper.

Lon and Laurie spread it out before Grandpa. Half of the front page was filled with two pictures: Lon beside the duck pen, and the enlarged footprint left by the prankster.

"That print's a hoax," Grandpa said.

"Was your boy's story of seeing a monster a practical joke too?" Lt. Raff asked.

Grandpa look at Lon.

"I saw something real," Lon insisted. He felt uncomfortable at the doubt on their faces.

"Hunters have fanned out through the woods now, searching for an ape-man or swamp-ape," Lt. Raff said. "Trouble is, some hunter may get trigger happy and shoot another person by mistake."

Grandpa frowned. "I wish we'd never called Animal Control," he said, "or told anyone about—whatever it is. Next time we'll know better. You kids remember—monsters and oil wells don't mix!"

"We sure will," Lon agreed. He was worried. He didn't want anyone to be accidentally shot because he had told about seeing the strange creature.

Lt. Raff put a megaphone to his lips and called a warning to the people spread out through the woods. "This 'ape' could be a person who's living in the wild, a hermit. If you shoot such a man or woman, you'll be held for murder."

"No matter what it is, I don't want it killed," Lon said.

"I hope no one shoots," Lt. Raff agreed. "If there is such a thing, it hasn't bothered anyone."

Again Lon felt ashamed, as if he had made up a story which no one believed. He wasn't a hoaxster, but he felt like one when the officer looked at him in this way.

"Let's go find Jane," Laurie said.

As they walked across the yard, a man stopped them. He wore a big straw hat that hadn't kept his skin from burning dark as leather, and his stomach bulged over his belt. Lon felt that he had seen the big man someplace before.

"You the kid that saw the ape-man?" he asked.

Lon nodded.

"Well," the man said, "I'm always looking for a new attraction for my wild animal show. I run a fishing camp on the highway, where the river crosses. Sell stuff to tourists. Caged animals bring in lots of customers."

Lon knew him then. Once he and Mother had stopped at the camp when their car needed gas. He could never forget the smell of the cages on that hot day, or the animals pacing back and forth behind iron bars, their tongues hanging out. Over and over they tried to find a crack big enough to escape to the wild where they belonged.

"You kids can make some money," the man said. "Just call me at the camp if you see that monster again."

Neither Laurie or Lon said a word as the man hurried to rejoin the hunt. Then Lon said, "I wouldn't tell him anything."

"No," Laurie agreed. "I don't want any creature put in a cage."

They found Jane Kimball sitting with other young women and men under a tree.

"Is your well water safe to drink?" a boy asked.

"We only use it for the house," Lon said. "Grandpa brings our drinking water in gallon jugs from a spring a couple of miles down the road."

"If you're thirsty," Laurie said, "I'll get you water." She ran to the house.

Two of the boys were tuning guitars. Jane hummed into a harmonica.

"Are you going to sleep in your tree-tent tonight?" Lon asked her.

"Yes," she said. "We put it up about a half mile into the swamp. But no use going in until evening."

"Meanwhile might as well enjoy," one of the boys said. He twanged the strings and began to make up a song:

"Ape man's been here.
Huntin's on,

But not for me, not for me.
Let him live. Let him live.
Have a holiday.
Enjoy!"

He had a good voice, but Lon didn't see how he could sing when so many hunters were out after the monster.

"I don't want it killed," he said to Jane.

"I don't either," she said. "Whatever it is, it's survived all these years in the wild. It has to be a rare species, some creature almost extinct. It would be a crime to kill it for no reason."

Laurie returned with a glass jug of water. It passed quickly from person to person.

"We want to stay overnight with you in the tree-tent," Laurie told Jane, "but Mother hasn't come home. If we ask Grandpa, he'll probably say no."

"Grandpa's good to us," Lon hastened to add, "but he's upset about the crowd. He says monsters and oil wells don't mix."

Jane smiled. "Your Grandpa's nice," she said. "We got along fine after I bandaged his hand. Tell him I need you for company."

"Then maybe he'll let us go," Lon said.

"Let's find him," Laurie said. "We might as well know one way or the other."

They did not see him among the people in the yard. He didn't answer when Laurie called at the door of the motor home.

Then they heard him tramping through the bush and ran to meet him beside the duck pen.

"I covered up that prankster's false footprint," he said. "If anyone found it, we'd never get people out of here."

"Grandpa," Laurie said. "Jane's asked us to sleep over in her tree-tent tonight."

"You don't mean that crowd's planning to stay all night!" Grandpa cried in alarm.

Lon said hurriedly, "Only Jane. She's writing about strange creatures seen in America."

"For the university," Laurie added, for Grandpa respected an education.

"You mean that sensible girl *believes* in monsters?" Grandpa asked.

"She said it might be an important living link to the past," Laurie explained.

"She has a pup-tent on a platform high in a tree in the swamp," Lon added hopefully. "We'd take our sleeping bags and be perfectly safe up there with Jane."

"You saw how efficient she was when she bandaged your hand," Laurie pleaded.

Grandpa looked at them and said nothing. They knew that he always hated to say no, when they really wanted to do something.

"The creature I saw didn't try to hurt me when we were face to face," Lon said.

Suddenly Grandpa seemed to make up his mind. "Lon," he said, "can't be sure that what you saw wasn't a shadow from a tree swayed by the wind. Or from a cloud moving across the moon. Shadows plus imagination can turn into odd shapes in the night."

Lon knew it wasn't a shadow, but this was no time to say so.

"Maybe," Grandpa said, "if you stay overnight, you'll prove to yourself that there's nothing unusual living in the swamp. Jane seems a reliable girl. She's old enough to be through college, and a tent high in a tree should be safe. Besides, the three of you would leave a trail, going in, that I could easily follow if you were lost."

"Then we can go!" Laurie cried and gave him a quick hug.

"Thank you, Grandpa," Lon said.

He thought if Laurie and Jane saw the creature, too, Grandpa would no longer doubt his story.

6
All
Night in a
Tree-Tent

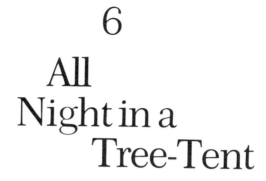

Late in the day the crowd began to thin out. Lt. Raff was doing his best to get stragglers to leave.

"You can't stay here all night," he warned through his megaphone. "This is private property. There are no facilities. Already you've used all the drinking water Mr. Regan had for the weekend. Let's go along home and leave this family in peace."

The young people with Jane told her good-bye. "If you don't come back," one of the boys teased, "can I have your old jeep?"

"Shut up, Frank," another boy said. "If we haven't the courage to stay overnight in that swamp, we can at least wish *her* luck."

Jane laughed and waved as they left. She turned to Laurie and Lon, "I hope you're coming with me," she said. "I don't feel as brave as I thought I'd be."

"Grandpa said we could go," Laurie said. "We've made peanut butter sandwiches and some of cheese. They'll keep safely even in the heat."

"We have to get them and our sleeping bags," Lon said. "And I'll lock up. Grandpa's gone to the spring for more drinking water. He filled our canteens before he left."

"Mother might come back while he's gone," Laurie said. "We better leave her a note."

It would take too much time for a long explanation, so Lon wrote on a sheet of paper and left it on the kitchen table: "Grandpa will tell you where we are."

Jane led the way, walking into the swamp. Laurie and Lon followed single file with packs on their backs.

This was not the kind of woods where one could take a pleasant walk, Lon thought, dropping a few paces behind the girls. He and Laurie loved to walk under the long needle pine and live oak which bordered the road, but here they had to watch where they were going, step from one hummock of spongy earth to another.

Between hummocks, great gnarled roots of cypress trees buried themselves in stagnant pools of green water. At first there were surprises of single wild flower plants where enough sun filtered through the tangled branches to help them bloom. Something soft and smothering dropped onto Lon's

face. He grabbed it and threw it from him. It was only a beard of gray Spanish moss.

As they walked on, the woods grew deeper and darker and underneath the trees only green moss and tall ferns grew. Here and there the ferns were trampled by the passing of some wild creature.

Lon sniffed the strange smell of stale water, crushed lush green plants, and old rotting wood. A screech from above his head startled him. He saw Jane and Laurie stop, too.

"Only a fish hawk," Lon called.

"The tree-tent's here," Jane said.

Lon looked about at the lonely, wild place. Maybe this was the way the whole world was in the beginning, he thought. It was almost as dark as evening.

"What time is it?" he asked. "Night yet?"

"About seven," Jane said. "It won't be sundown for an hour."

She started to climb a rope ladder hanging from a great old tree.

"You thought of everything," Lon said.

He followed Laurie up the ladder and came upon the tree-tent hidden among leafy vines. They ducked their heads and crawled in through the open flap of the tent. It was like being in a small, dark cave.

"It's a tight fit with our sleeping bags," Jane said, "but none of us is very big."

56

On her knees, Laurie's head barely touched the top of the tent. "How did you find such a secret spot?" she whispered, for it seemed the kind of place to whisper.

"Well," Jane said, "I figured if I were an ape-man with hunters after me, this is where I'd choose to hide."

"You're right," Lon said, wiping sweat from his forehead. "There can't be a wilder place in this swamp, or a hotter place either."

"When the seabreeze comes up," Jane said, "it will cool us."

"If a breeze can get through the tops of these trees," Lon said.

Laurie gave a cry and drew away from a big spider running up the side of the tent. "I'm not really afraid," she apologized. "It startled me."

"At least we didn't see a snake," Lon said.

Jane took a bottle of insect repellent from her back-pack. "Here, rub some on you," she said. "Mosquitoes are worse to sleep with than spiders."

The odor of citronella filled the tent. They wiped their hands on paper napkins before unwrapping and eating the sandwiches, and drinking the orange juice they had brought with them.

In contrast to the dark in the tent, the woods outside now seemed in half light. Jane reached in her pocket for her harmonica, then thought better of it.

"If something is near," she said, "I don't want to

frighten it away."

"Let's tell stories," Laurie said. "You tell us, Jane, about some of the strange creatures that people have seen, the ones you are writing your thesis about."

"Yes," Lon said. "You never told us about the man you said was kidnapped by an ape-man a long time ago. I forgot his name."

"Ostman," Jane said. "It happened fifty years ago, but my grandfather remembers it. Ostman was prospecting for gold on an island. He said a giant creature, eight feet tall, came in the night and picked him up in his sleeping bag and carried him off into the deep woods."

Lon looked at his own sleeping bag and the back of his neck prickled.

"What did he do?" Laurie asked. "He must have escaped if he lived to tell it."

"He did escape," Jane said, "but not for several days. He lived in the woods with the ape-man and a female and their smaller son. They ate roots and plants. They seemed able to communicate with each other in grunts and other sounds. They didn't hurt him. They only seemed very interested in whatever he did. They watched him curiously, the way we'd watch them, and they tried to imitate him."

"Did Ostman have a gun?" Lon asked.

"I don't know," Jane said. "I don't think he'd

want to shoot them if he did. He said they seemed more like hairy men from prehistoric times than like animals."

Lon lay on top of his sleeping bag, with a flashlight beside him. "The creature I saw," he said, "could easily pick up all three of us and carry us away."

Laurie yawned. "I'm really sleepy. Wake me if anything happens."

Lon thought she must be pretending not to be a little anxious, but she slept at once.

Jane placed her camera with flash attachment near her hand and lay down, too.

Lon wondered if she could really sleep. His own mind was racing with the excitement of the day and the anticipation of the night. He could hear every small sound, the croaking of tree frogs, the scuttle of little feet on the bark of the tree. Wood mice? Tree lizards? What might live deep in the swamp?

The tree was tall. The wooden platform under the tent was strong. He wasn't afraid, he told himself. He was only tuned, listening, waiting for any happening at all.

He must have dozed, for suddenly he was wide awake, and he knew that time had passed. He didn't know what had waked him. Perhaps a dream. A sound? Or did he just feel something?

He lay perfectly still, his heart beating hard.

Carefully he felt for his flashlight, but he did not turn it on.

Neither Laurie nor Jane moved. Everything was quiet.

Then he felt a kind of motion in the dark. Had a seabreeze come up? Had it moved across his hands and face to wake him?

He sat up slowly and listened. The gray light of the woods showed through the open flap of the tent. Five minutes passed and his heart slowed its beating.

Then he heard Jane sit up suddenly. "Lon," she whispered.

"Sh-h-h," he said.

She leaned across Laurie to speak in his ear. "You didn't hear a thing—and yet you heard something? Right?"

"Yes," he said.

"Me, too," she breathed.

They waited. Not a sound. Even the tree frogs had stopped their croaking song.

Then from below, at the foot of the tree, came a sound of scratching, not a mouse this time. Not a lizard. Deep scratching as a giant cat might sharpen its claws against bark.

"A wildcat?" Jane whispered.

"Maybe," Lon said.

Laurie turned over and made a sleepy sound. Lon gripped her arm. "Sh-h-h," he said in her ear.

She sat up.

They heard it breathing then. Deep, heavy breathing that had to come from powerful lungs. It was more frightening than any growl or snarl could be.

"Did you pull up the rope ladder?" Lon whispered.

"No," Jane said. "I thought we might need it in a hurry."

"We do," Laurie said, "but something's at the bottom of it. Do you think it can climb?"

Lon did not answer. He was already at the entrance of the tent, feeling in the darkness for the top of the ladder. Jane was beside him. They found it and began to pull. It would not come. Something held onto it at the other end.

Suddenly the tent swayed as if the tree had been shaken.

Jane said, "I'm pulling the ladder as hard as I can. It won't budge."

Lon reached for his flashlight. He shone it directly at the bottom of the tree. A great shadow moved. Nothing he could actually see. The rope ladder came up so quickly that Jane fell backward into the tent with it. Startled, Lon dropped his flashlight. It shone dimly in the tall fern below.

Then there was a scream, high pitched and angry, like nothing Lon had ever heard before. It was louder than the scream of a panther, which he

had heard once in the Everglades. It was much louder than a raccoon. It was a frustrated cry of rage from a great throat.

The creature went on chattering and scolding as if Jane and Lon had pulled away something it wanted very much.

Lon and Laurie and Jane were frozen with shock. They didn't know how long it was until the woods grew quiet again. Finally Laurie spoke.

"Something was there, Jane," she said, "and you forgot to take a picture."

"I never thought of the camera," Jane admitted. "I was scared to death."

"I still am," Lon said. "How long is it until morning?"

Jane turned the flashlight on her wristwatch. "The sun will be up in a couple of hours," she said. "And I'm glad you kids are with me. I didn't think I could be so terrified."

"There should be footprints below," Lon said, "when it's light enough for us to go home."

But when they climbed down the ladder, they found that the crushed ferns below were too thick for footprints to show.

"It's like walking on a mattress," Jane said.

"I can't find my flashlight," Lon said, feeling among the ferns. "I could see it here last night."

"Because it was lighted," Jane said. "The battery probably burned out."

"Look here!" Laurie cried. She was on her knees before a spongy moss hummock. They knelt beside her.

At first Lon could see only a puddle of water the size of a dinner plate on the green moss. Then he realized that, under the clear water, the bottom was shaped like a big foot. Four thick toes extended from a round center.

"Like the print in the garden," Laurie whispered.

"And the one we saw on the beach," Lon said.

"It's a perfect footprint or pawprint," Jane said as if she couldn't believe what she saw "Water has risen to fill it, but the print held its shape."

"Can you get a picture?" Lon asked.

Jane's hands shook with excitement as she adjusted the camera for flash. She snapped shots from several angles directly above it.

"I hope I got the shape of the print through the water," she said. "Now both of you place your hands on the moss by the side of the puddle, and

spread your fingers. I want to show the difference in size."

When she put her camera back into its case, Lon said, "Jane, you won't give these to the newspapers, will you? Grandpa will really be angry if any more crowds come near his rig."

"No one will hear a word from me until my thesis is published," Jane promised, "and that will take a long time, a year or two. Then these pictures will bring scientists here."

Lon frowned. "We don't want hunters again."

"Don't worry," Jane said. "Scientists won't tell. They don't want the few remaining strange creatures killed any more than we do. Such an important link to the past is as valuable to scientists as your grandpa's oil wells are to him."

"Jane," Laurie asked, "will you come back here again tonight and hope to see it?"

"Not for anything," Jane said. "I never again want to be that frightened. I'm convinced it was there. That will have to be enough for me."

"I still wish I could see it," Lon said, "but not here at night."

They searched again for Lon's flashlight, but it was gone. "Probably sunk in the mud," he said.

They went out of the swamp much faster than they had gone in. The sun was shining on Jane's jeep, parked at the roadside, as they told her good-bye.

"My friends will come back to help me get the tent and ladder," she said. "I know I can trust you not to tell a word of what happened."

"We won't," Laurie said.

"Never," Lon agreed. "No one except Grandpa and Mother, and they'll never tell."

When she had gone, the twins turned toward the motor home. Their mother's car was parked in the dirveway. They entered the house quietly, in case she was asleep.

They were tip-toeing around the kitchen, frying eggs and making toast, when she woke. She came in her pink dressing gown, smiling.

"Did you see Mr. Carter?" Lon asked. Somehow he was not ready to talk about their night in the swamp. It was hard enough for him to believe. He didn't want to be told again that shadows plus imagination formed strange shapes.

"You had the right idea," she said happily. "Mr. Carter was glad to help us. We found all except five of the landowners and signed them up."

Lon felt relieved and thankful. After all their hard work and expense, Grandpa and his partners would get back their money and more.

Grandpa waked and came from his room. "I'd like to see Trevor Tate's face Monday morning when he goes to the County Clerk's office and finds that we beat him to the list and the leases," he said.

Lon grinned. "You said you'd scramble that tough egg," he said, "and you did."

Grandpa Regan nodded. Lon had never seen him look happier. "We're really on top of oil this time, kids," he said. "Wait until you see the latest sample that Ned assayed. It's reeking with crude."

"Great," Lon said. "Can we be there when you bring in the well?"

"I wouldn't let you miss it," Grandpa promised, "but there are days of work yet to complete it. We don't want to waste a drop of oil in a gusher. After we test its pressure, we'll bring in special equipment to control the flow from the well. Then the company that buys our leases will build surface dams and reservoirs and pipelines to protect the surrounding land from oil contamination."

Lon whistled. "All that work just to get going?" he asked.

His mother laughed. "Plenty of work and excitement for all of us for months ahead," she said.

Suddenly Grandpa seemed to remember that Lon and Laurie had been gone overnight. "How about you two?" he asked. "Did you find that tree-tent so comfortable that you want to move there permanently?"

Laurie shook her head.

Lon said, "Something big was there."

Grandpa's face turned an angry red. "You're not starting that all over again!" he said. "I won't have more publicity, and strangers swarming all over the place with all we have at stake."

"Papa, wait!" their mother said. "Lon wouldn't make up a story after what happened here yesterday."

She turned to the twins. "Tell us. Did you actually *see* it?"

"Not really *see* it," Lon said. "We *heard* it."

"It was so mad when Jane and Lon pulled the rope ladder away," Laurie added.

Together they told of the night in the tree-tent, one remembering what the other had left out. "I'll never forget its angry scream," Lon ended. "If I hadn't dropped my flashlight, I might have seen it then."

"When we climbed down the ladder in the morning," Laurie added, "we almost missed the footprint it left. Swamp water had covered it."

"Good," Grandpa said. "Another print is all we need to bring that crowd back on us again!"

"That's what we decided, too," Lon said. "Jane says this creature may be as important to scientists as your oil well is to you. We don't want hunters to kill it, or someone to shut it in a cage."

"Whatever is in the swamp," Laurie added, "we want it to *live*."

"I just hope it feels the same way about us," Lon said, "and stays in the swamp where it belongs."

7

The
Monster

Before Grandpa went to the rig the next morning, he called Lon and Laurie to him. "No more visits into the swamp now, you hear?"

Lon said nothing. He had never been afraid of any creature before, and he didn't like the feeling.

"I'm going into town with Mother to buy new clothes," Laurie said. "School starts Monday."

"You've out-grown everything this summer," their mother said. "Lon, don't you want to come, too? I can guess at your shirt and jeans sizes, but not shoes."

"Those sneakers that were too big for me fit now," he said. "I want to go fishing. When school starts, I'll only have Saturdays and Sundays free."

His mother smiled as if she understood how he felt. "All right," she said. "Make the most of your last day of vacation. Can I count on fish for supper?"

As soon as they had gone Lon took a handful of

peanuts in case he met the squirrel again on the path beside the cypress swamp. For himself he stuffed a big red apple into his hip pocket. A crisp, juicy apple, the first of the fall crop which his mother had found on the market.

He stepped out of the door and felt a deep quietness around him. He had never been entirely alone here before. He liked the stillness and peace. Even the ducks were dozing under the tree that sheltered them from the hot sun.

He carried a can and spade to dig worms for bait in a shaded place he knew. When he pulled back the ferns, a bright green lizard ran up his arm, stopped at his elbow and looked at him without fear. Lon laughed.

The tiny lizard was only one of many wild friends he had made since he came here. A mocking bird scolded and flew from the pine overhead. He looked up to see if she had a nest hidden there. If she did, the thick branches kept her secret.

With the can of worms in a plastic pail and a cane pole, he started down the path toward the creek that drained from the swamp into the Gulf waters. Often he had caught bream in the pools of black water where the creek spread wide through the roots of old cypress trees.

Carefully he stepped from one great gnarled root to another until he reached a pool ringed with reeds. The squirrel did not come to meet him today. None of the usual small animals seemed to be here. No frogs, turtles, wood mice or raccoons. Yet he saw nothing to frighten them away.

Downstream, a great blue heron stood on long thin legs and watched him bait his hook. She wanted fish to eat, too. Careful not to make a sound he adjusted a red and white cork to the three-foot depth of water and dropped in his line and hook.

It had scarecely sunk when the bobbing cork was dragged under. Lon lifted on the cane pole and brought out a fat bream, just the size that Mother split and baked with a slice of lemon and dressing on top. He was hungry thinking about it.

Each time he baited the hook and cast, a bream took it under. He stopped when he had four in the plastic pail. He wanted only enough for supper. Then he remembered that Ned might return with Grandpa, so he caught a fifth fish.

While he bent his head to take the fish from the hook, the great blue heron slipped up behind him and helped herself to a bream from the pail. He turned to see her swallowing the fish whole, head-first. He shooed her away with a wave of his hand.

She flew with such a flapping of wings that she startled a colony of white ibis searching for craw-fish downstream. Noisily they rose above the trees as Lon watched. How beautiful they were with their black-tipped white wings spread a yard wide.

They flew over so close that he could see their bright orange-red feet.

While he was catching a fish to replace the one the heron had stolen, a bright flash of light blinded him for a moment, then was gone. It was like the glint of sun reflected on a mirror. He tried to see what had caused it.

He squinted at patches of blue sky through the treetops, then at a thick, twisted vine hanging almost to the ground from the trunk of a baldheaded cypress a few yards away. Nothing unusual.

Now that the ibis and heron had gone, an unearthly stillness settled over the pool. He wiped sweat from his forehead, swatted a mosquito and decided to go home. He must clean the fish and put them in the refrigerator.

He felt really hungry now and took the big red apple from his pocket. He bit through its crisp peel and juice spurted out. Good!

A flash of light blinded him again. This time he knew that it came from the top of the old bald cypress. He looked up, and there was the monster he had seen at the duck pen. The monster he had heard last night beneath the tree-tent. It had to be the same creature, for it held Lon's flashlight in its hairy hand. The glint of sun against the shiny sides of the flashlight reflected into Lon's eyes.

Lon stood motionless, holding the apple to his mouth, and stared. He wasn't frightened this time.

He was only fascinated by this unusual creature so near him.

The monster was sitting on the flat top of the old trunk as if it sat on a chair, its legs crossed, comfortable and casual. It was completely absorbed in examining the flashlight, which it must have carried since last night.

Lon was afraid to move or make a sound. He might scare it away. The monster looked a little like pictures he had seen of chimpanzees, only its head was not flat, but dome-shaped like a human head. In daylight, it was not as big as he had thought, more the size of Mother than Grandpa. It was covered with short brown hair except for smooth pinkish brown skin on its face and the palms of its hands. Its feet, hanging over the crown of the tree, were big, four times as large as its hands.

It looked closely at one end of the flashlight, then tipped the case over and stared into the other end. Finally it shook the light as a child might shake a rattle.

Suddenly it saw Lon and it frowned, then hugged the flashlight to its chest as if Lon had tried to take it away.

"You can keep it," Lon called, before he realized that he was talking to the monster as if it could understand him.

It looked at him intently. Its brown eyes seemed curious and as interested in him as he was in it.

Then Lon realized that it was really looking at his big red apple. Could the monster catch the apple if he threw it up there? Lon decided to try. First, he tossed the apple into the air and caught it in one hand. "See?" he called.

The monster tipped its head to one side. Its pointed ears stood straight up.

"Catch," Lon called and threw the apple.

The monster watched but let the apple go by him. It fell into the weeds beside the pool. In seconds the big creature slid down the tree trunk, still holding the flashlight in one hand. With the other he snatched the apple from the weeds. He turned it slowly until he had examined all sides. He sniffed it, then took half of the apple in one bite. He chewed, testing the taste.

"It's good, isn't it?" Lon called as if talking to a friend.

The monster hid the apple behind its back, then quickly disappeared into the deep swamp.

Lon stood there for a moment, wondering if he could be dreaming. Of course he wasn't, he decided. His apple was gone.

He picked up the pail of fish and cane pole and started home. He was happy again. What an experience to tell Grandpa and Mother and Laurie tonight. Even if his mother suggested that clouds, hot sun, shadows and a vivid imagination might have something to do with what he had seen, he knew better.

He didn't know what it was – swamp-ape, ape-man, big-foot. But it had trusted him enough to eat his apple. Lon knew that he had made a new friend at the edge of the swamp today, and he would never be afraid of monsters again.